Because bear skin needs protection.

HunkaBear

The first issue in a collection of porcelain figurines portraying favorite brawny bruins.

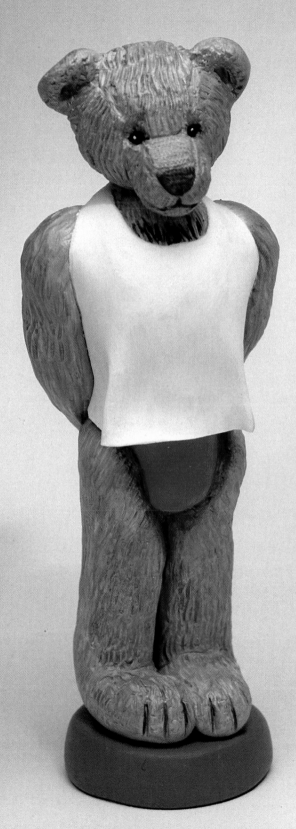

Inspired by the variety of hirsute hunks, the Danbeary Mint has created *HunkaBear*. Like its forebears, this unique character has been sculpted of fine porcelain. His masterful features have been painted by paw. Indeed, every detail— from muscles to muzzle— has been carefully bestowed to create this honey of a bear.

Handsomely endowed with a white strap undershirt and Calvin Ursine designer briefs, *HunkaBear* is the bear essence of beefcake. This ursa major will make your honey hot.

An exceptional value

HunkaBear is available exclusively from the Danbeary Mint. He can be all yours for just $49, payable in two monthly installments of $24.50 each. This attractive price also includes a felt base protector. Send no money now! Simply return the Reservation Application. You can charge your *HunkaBear* on American BearCard or Master CubCard.

Your satisfaction is guaranteed. You may return your figurine within 30 days for replacement or refund. What's more, owners of *HunkaBear* will have the privilege of possessing the other brawny bruins in the series as they become available. This collection of teddy bear figurines is sure to become a bearloom.

HunkaBear's masterful facial features are expertly painted by paw.

HunkaBear's chest hairs are expertly painted by paw.

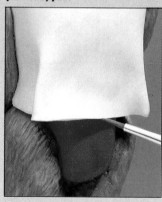

HunkaBear's undershirt and designer briefs are expertly painted by paw.

ON THE COVER

Bearethtaking cover model, Columbine, created by Ted Menten. Dressed in diamonds from Van Cleef and Arbears and wearing an Yves Saint Bearent gown.

Copyright © 1988 by Ted Menten.
Printed in Hong Kong. All rights reserved under the Pan-American and International Copyright Conventions.

Canadian representatives: General Publishing Co., Ltd., 30 Lesmill Road, Don Mills, Ontario M3B 2T6.

International representatives: Worldwide Media Services, Inc., 115 East Twenty-third Street, New York, NY 10010.

9 8 7 6 5 4 3 2 1

Digit on the right indicates the number of this printing.

Library of Congress Cataloging-in-Publication Number 88-42753

ISBN 0-89471-637-9

Cover photograph by Ted Menten

Cover design by Ted Menten

Printed by South Sea International Press, Ltd.

Typography by Today's Graphics, Inc.

This book may be ordered by mail from the publisher. Please include $1.50 for postage. *But try your bookstore first!*
Running Press Book Publishers
125 South Twenty-second Street
Philadelphia, Pennsylvania 19103

TEDDY'S BEARZAAR

written, photographed and designed by
TED MENTEN
additional features written by
C.E. CRIMMINS and STEVE ZORN
illustrations by
JUNE AMOS GRAMMER

Arctophile

THE INSTINCT FOR THE BEAR ESSENCE

HOUBEARGANT • PARIS

Bear Blass

*The news is black and white:
the look of pandas—short,
full and striped matched to
cropped, small, and pearled.
Couture Cub Salon.*

*The Panda Style: Pearled mock-bolero jacket
over ruffled horizontal panels of organza,
in black and white. A honey of a price at $3500.00.*

Neiman-Bearcus

In a world brimming with questions
one ladybear puts an answer to every query

Dear Abear

Abigail Van Bruin writes a syndicated advice column that appears daily in over three hundred newspapers across America. Her special warmth and cuddlesome charm make even the most difficult problems bearable.

Dear Abear:
   One of my snobby neighbors claims that her forebears from England are the real original teddy bears. I am of German extraction and come from a long line of Steiffs. To the best of my knowledge I am a descendant of the original clan.

                    —In a Quandary

Dear In a Quandary:
   Much mystery and confusion surrounds the origin of the first teddy bear clan, but one thing is sure, they did not come from England! There is some evidence that indicates that your ancestors date from the early 1900s, possibly before 1902. However, they were simply referred to as toy bears. Then, in 1903, when the American President Teddy Roosevelt refused to shoot a bear cub and Clifford Berryman drew the immortal cartoon entitled "Drawing the Line in Mississippi," there developed a new trend calling toy bears *Teddy's bear,* which later was shortened to *teddy bear.*
   Both the German toy company Steiff and the American toy company Ideal claim to have designed the original teddy bear. Since "teddy bear" is a generic term that cannot be copyrighted or patented, the point seems moot.

Dear Abear:
   I'm at a rather swanky dinner party. The gentlebear across the table from me (let's call him Ben) has a rather conspicuous glob of honey dangling from one of his whiskers. Considering that Ben and I have met only this evening, would it seem overbearing for me to tell him about it, or should I just ignore it and hope the problem corrects itself?

                    —Grizzelda

Dear Grizzelda:
   By all means tell him, but don't cause a scene (for instance, *never* lean across the table and lick it off yourself).

Dear Abear:
   Are stitched noses more fashionable than molded ones?

                    —Nosey

Dear Nosey:
   Yes—and prettier, too. Mine is rust brown.

Dear Abear:
   I never thought I'd be writing to you, but I really need your help. I'm ashamed to admit it, but I think I have a serious pill problem. You see, like my forebears, my plush is not a very high-quality acrylic. Years of hugging and cuddling have made my fuzz bunch up into little pills. They practically cover my bearskin. Is there anything I can do to refurbish my fur?

                    —Fuzzy Wuzzy

Dear FW:
   Don't despair, dear bear. Just be thankful you've enjoyed all those years of affectionate hugging. I'll bet nobody even notices your pilling problem. But if it still bothers you, why not invest in one of those gadgets that whisks off bothersome pills quickly and painlessly?

Dear Abear:
   I am a teddy bear interested in astrology. Please tell me how to determine my moment of birth so that I can cast my horoscope.

                    —Starry-eyed

Dear Starry-eyed:
   My good friend and wise astrologer, Ursa Beara, has the correct answer to your question. According to her, a teddy bear is *born* the moment it is loved.

Dear Abear:
   How many times has this happened to you? You're riding the bus and next to you is a rather well-dressed bruin—except he has this tiny little thread sticking out of his sleeve. All you can think about is pulling that piece of thread. You believe this bear brummel type would appreciate the removal of this blot on his wardrobe, so you reach out to pull the thread. Next thing you know, his arm falls off. It was a loose seam. What a faux paw —I've never been so embearassed!

                    —Paws to Yourself

Dear Paws:
   This has never happened to me.

Dear Abear:
   My fur is made of a synthetic fibre often referred to as plush. My neighbor's fur is a natural fibre called mohair and I am told that it is made from goat hair. She is a rather hightoned bear and her attitude toward me is that my fur is of inferior grade.

                    —Feeling Second-Class

Dear Feeling Second-Class:
   A well-designed cotton dress is still more fashionable than a poorly designed brocaded one. While mohair is usually more expensive because it is imported, there are many new synthetic fibre plushes being imported that are every bit as lush and every bit as expensive. Like any true classical item of fashion, the design and not the fabric is what wins kudos.

Dear Abear:
   My human companion was distressed recently because someone called him an *Arctophile.* Was this an insult?

                    —Curious Cub

Dear Curious:
   Heavens no! An arctophile is a person who loves teddy bears. Groups of teddy bear lovers are referred to as arctophilists or arctophiles. While these words are not in the dictionary, they are in common usage and are respectful approbations.

In the beginning,
Tedée Lauder created Bear Definer.

Now the evolution: Tedée Lauder's new
Bear Definer/Duo

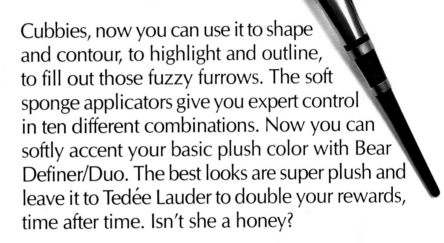

Cubbies, now you can use it to shape
and contour, to highlight and outline,
to fill out those fuzzy furrows. The soft
sponge applicators give you expert control
in ten different combinations. Now you can
softly accent your basic plush color with Bear
Definer/Duo. The best looks are super plush and
leave it to Tedée Lauder to double your rewards,
time after time. Isn't she a honey?

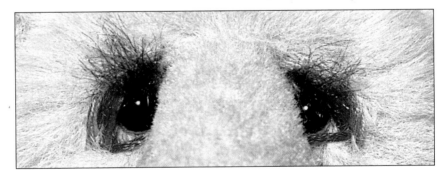

TEDĒE
LAUDER

NEW YORK · LONDON · PARIS · BERLIN

YvesSaintBearent

With the return of intriguing necklines and the look of bare plush comes the return of pearls—for day or night. It's unbearably brilliant! Pearls became bearish in the 1960s, but now they're back, real and faux, as the bear market choice of today.

PEARLY PASSIONS

Have pearls replaced diamonds as a girlbear's best friend?

Pearls have been in for centuries but, given the rarity of fine, natural specimens, they were historically the domain of royalty and the very rich. Today, happily, all that has changed. If you're made simply bearethless by the lustre of pearls, you've landed in the right century. For this is the era of the faultless faux gem. Coco Cubnel mixes pearls with gold chains over a black velvet cap to recreate the romantic look of Juliet. Polara Picasso creates a dynamic statement with her oversized ear baubles that even young cubbies can afford.

A plethora of pearls cascading down the back, *above*, at Bearlenciaga; *left*, Bearry Ellis creates clusters of pearls for the neck and ears. The most unusual embellishment—a simple strand of pearls entwined in a shoulder strap, ending in a rosebud at the back. The strand exclusively at Bloomingbruins, New York.

All the drama of Shakesbear's romance as **Coco Cubnel creates a black velvet and pearl trimmed Juliet's cap, *left*. Oversized art deco ear ornaments, *right*, by Polara Picasso** are this season's bear market prime choice.

In or out of style, pearls have always had their champions. In 1970, Mrs. Whitney Astor Vanderbear fell so passionately in love with a $1.2 million double strand of pearls spotted at Van Cub and Arpels that she decided to trade in her magnificent collection of Viennese honey pots to own them. Today, the faux version, *above*, can be had for a price anyone can bear.

It happens in every relationship—you and your bearloved start growling at each other for no reason at all. Soon you're climbing the den walls, clawing at each other's throats. No, you haven't fallen out of love, you've just gotten in a rut. You've got cabin fever, a bad case of Lover's Clawstrophobia.

The only solution? A trip for just the two of you, a romantic sojourn where you'll strip away the layers of high-stress living to rediscover each other's bear essence.

The Love Journey— On the Prowl for Romance

By C.E. Crimmins

Where to go? Well, almost anywhere will do. Remember, it's the spirit and not the destination that counts. But it doesn't hurt to try some spectacular locations. The bear mention of these locations conjures up romantic images:

BEAR RIVER, UTAH For wilderness lovers who can bear a lot of excitement, how about a whitewater rafting trip down this perilous river? Rapid water leads to a rapid heartbeat, and we all know what a heartthrob a guy becomes when he's back to nature, battling the elements.

By day, watch your man-cub put pad to paddle and navigate the river. Sit bearlegged on the side of the boat and thrill to the spectacular scenery. By night, snuggle with your honey under the stars. It's probably been years since you've seen the Milky Way, the Big Dipper, and, of course, Ursa Major, the Great Bear.

It's a trip that two starry-eyed lovers will never forget.

CLUB TED Located in sunny Bearmuda, this enchanting establishment is perfect for lovers who want to get away from it all.

Enjoy a casual poolside lunch of pawpaws, that delicious tropical fruit. Sip honeydew daiquiris while the sun sets over your thatched cottage.

The special things about Club Ted are its ordinary charms—a bearfoot stroll on the sandy beach, a bearback ride through the dunes. You'll unwind, let your fur down. Romance can't help but revive in the warmth of this tropical playground.

BEAR HARBOR, MAINE Take a second honeymoon trip to this New England village that bears a long tradition of Yankee hospitality. If teddy's an antique lover (or an antique himself!) he'll love prowling the quaint shops for a salt-glazed honeypot or an oriental rug for his den. Browse among fine woolens or scrimshaw. It's a shopper's paradise, and neither of you will go home bearhanded.

But don't neglect the area's natural charms. In spring the fragrance of old-fashioned honeysuckle fills the air. You'll want to stay in a charming inn overlooking the Atlantic, where the sound of waves crashing on the rocks will soothe the savage beast in your bruin.

And when you find your tummies growling, don't forget the famous Bear Harbor lobster feasts—cuisine to cuddle by!

Love on the Home Front

Is leaving your den unbearable or impossible right now? Don't denigrate the idea of staying put—it can be unbearably romantic!

Pre-Hibernation Love Feasts

After the hustle and bustle of a growling work week, what could be more relaxing—and romantic—than a cozy dinner for two in the privacy of your own den?

It needn't be elaborate, and even if your cupboard is bear, the ingredients for an elegant dinner for two can be assembled in minutes from your local supermarket or gourmet shop.

Atmosphere is all. Get rid of that harsh overhead lighting, banish bear bulbs—instead, set your table aglow with the soft shimmer of elegant beeswax candles. Turn off the tube and slip Beary Manilow into the CD player, or select a pleasing bearitone singer to set the mood. Classical fans could try a Bearlioz symphony. Finally, don't forget that fine fragrances make scents for any romantic occasion: A honeysuckle potpourri simmering on the stove will give your bruin a whiff of pleasures to come.

Simplicity is the bear essence of an alluring dinner. He'll want to cuddle between courses, not watch you clean dishes or assemble casseroles. So start with the simplest of appetizers, honey-roasted almonds, and a round of Ted's favorite cocktail, a Fuzzy Navel (peach schnapps and orange juice—a love potion ripe with possibilities!). There's no need to move to the table just yet. Let him relax, perhaps even put up his paws in the Bearcolounger before shifting into high flirtatious gear.

From here on, the meal is all sweetness and light. The main course? A salmon mousse with a rich béarnaise sauce, accompanied by fresh spears of asbearagus. To wash it down, choose a bottle of Teddy Bear Blush from one of several new boutique wineries in California. (Or, if you enjoy a drier vintage—how about a Beargundy?) You'll want to linger over this portion of the feast, where you'll bear witness to the aphrodisiacal qualities of fine food.

And now for a short and sweet finish—an array of desserts that'll set Ted's stomach a-growling once again. Let your sweet sentiments show by assembling a groaning board of delectables. You know he has a sweet tooth, so give him a whole larder to choose from. Yummy Gummi bears. Scrumptious honey-filled baklava from a Greek bakery. And lots of luscious berries that bears pick every time—raspberries, blueberries, blackberries. How about Strawbeary Shortcake? If you want to really show him you're sweet enough to melt in his mouth, splurge and order a box of chocolates with your image embossed on them. You'll finally find out fur sure if the way to his heart is through his tummy!

Finish your love feast snuggled together on the couch, sharing goblets of mead, history's most famous dessert wine. Made from honey, this delicious golden liquid was once enjoyed by medieval knights and their ladies. What better way to show him that his home is his castle, specially suited for the courtly rituals of love?

The Alfresco Alternative: Teddy Bear Picnic

Love blossoms out of doors, so when you and your bruin crave some fresh air in your relationship, take to the high road with a picnic lunch or dinner.

Honey-glazed chicken or ham are traditional picnic basket fare, but you might want to fan love's flames by planning an old-fashioned outdoor bearbeque. And why not tempt his tastebuds with some foreign touches? Marinated bamboo shoots will panda to his love of the exotic. Or shred some eucalyptus leaves and add mayonnaise for an excellent koala-slaw that will let him know he's your best mate.

Liz Claibear fragrance. A *grrreat* mood to be in.

Let it release the

RPELT

by Glorious Vanderpelt

bearness of you

BEARGDORF
GOODMAN

ON THE PLAZA IN NEW YORK

Calvin Ursine

A festive focus on eyes and nose tips for this season's most dramatic looks. Dazzle and delight as you cast aside the bear essentials!

FLAWLESS FACE

Being bearly beautiful isn't enough. When celebearations are in order you must step up the sizzle and put on a honey of a face.

This season's festive focus is on eyes and nose tips for the most dramatic looks.

● Treat yourself to new and imaginative makeup ideas. *Above*: Nose embroidery thread in a wide range of fashionable shades. *Far left*: Soft plush colors in champagne shades. Eyes lined with toned shades of cocoa brown. Nose tip color: Bearly Roseamber. *Top left*: Peachy-pink mohair fur accented with bearly darker nose tip shade—Peaches and Honey. *Below left*: Dramatic eye shadow created with a variety of embroidery thread colors, combined to create a honey of a look.

Pale plush is the secret to spectacular nighttime looks. It points up this season's bold eyes and nose tips. To achieve the effect, brush on eye shadow in thin layers—it mustn't look too painted. Nose-embroidery thread comes in a wide range of fashion colors. Choose those that highlight the eyes, but don't detract from the overall coloring of the face. Cream-colored bruins can accentuate beige-shaded eyes with a taupe or soft rust-colored nose tip. A peach-colored bear might select a roseamber shade.

BEAREST BREATH OF PERFECTION....

19

Tradition goes up in a puff of smoke as New York designers revolutionize evening wear. Options in colors and fabrics are unlimited: One can bearly make a choice!

opening nights

Brilliant solid colors play an important role on Broadway this season. When the house lights dim you'll continue to shine in bright satins and boastful taffetas in colors from pastel to bright. And look what's back: The vest!

STARSTRUCK ACTION! THIS COLORFUL CENTER STAGE ENSEMBLE BEARIGHTENS THE NIGHT. BRAVO!

Poofed satin skirt in emerald green cinched at the waist by a crimson samuri sash, *left,* is topped off with a bejeweled vest by Emanuel Unbearo. The look is hardly furtive and much too plush to be ignored. Fabulous faux furs by Bearglama complete the effect. Ear clips and choker by Fabeargé. Shimmering Shadows eye liner and plush blusher from the Elizabear Arden salon. Bring out the beast in your bruin!

SATIN FINISHES, VELVET CARESSES, AND GLITTERING GEMS, ALL MAKE A SPECTACULAR, STAR-STUDDED STATEMENT. WONDERBEAR!

Slinky black velvet dress trimmed with white satin ribbon oversized bow, *right,* by Calvin Ursine has all the ingredients of a show-stopper. Faux gems are a hit by Van Cleef & Arbears. Fur Tints by Cover Cub make even the most standoffish bruin feel cuddlesome.

SEASON SIZZLER. DIAMONDS AND A FLAME RED PARTY DRESS. TOO HOT TO HANDLE BUT TOO COOL TO RESIST. A BEARABLE BONFIRE! Red silk faille, bell-skirt dress with lace overlay by Bear Blass, *left*, will bearighten any season opener. Pale Ivory Blusher by Tedée Lauder makes even the palest fur look moondrenched. Be a flame in your bruin's fantasy!

EMBROIDERED SPLENDOR— BLACK TAFFETA TAKES A BOW TO THIS ONE-OF-A-KIND VEST. THIS STYLE IS URSA MAJOR! Hand-embroidered and beaded multi-colored evening vest, *inset right*, by Albeart Nipon. Worn over a black taffeta gown created by Georgio Bearmani. Ear ornaments by Polara Picasso. The moment is now—don't wait to see what's bruin.

24

teddy in a teddy

When saucy little fashionable bears danced the Charleston and the Teddy Bear Rag at the Ritz, all that came between them and indiscretion was a little bit of satin and lace known as a *teddy*.

Today that little undergarment appears to be showing on the outside as well as underneath as trendy little cubbies in the rock world appear publicly in their panties.

The bare beginnings of a beautiful idea—
From seductive teddy to provocative
bustier, these satin-smooth little
nothings, worn inside or out,
bear witness to the romance
of ribbons and lace.

FLUTTERY FLAMBOYANCE— A BEARRAGE OF FLATTERING FEATHERS
This frothy pink fantasy from Saint Bearent Rive Gauche. Dramatic jacket in rooster/ostrich available at Beargdorf Goodman. A furry fashion flurry in feathers!

As hemlines rise, knee-high skirts that flutter and flounce make their mark. Plushy little kneecaps are revealed. It's the season for fringes, feathers and froufrou!

FLASH
FEATHERS
& FRINGE

**A whirlwind of ideas is sweeping
the season—the new spirit for cubbies is
all-out fresh and frisky. The bear with flair
wraps herself in boas with bounce**

**PLUSH WITH PLUMES—
BEAR IN MIND THAT THIS
FEATHERY FANTASY MAY
BE MORE THAN
HE CAN BEAR.**
Ostrich with a hint of
glitter, *left*, by Paris
designer Bearlenciaga.
On top, a taupe sequined
strapless bustier. Below,
a flurry of feathers in
complementary shades.
Gold earrings—
sensational—by Bulbeari.
This combination is
guaranteed to keep him
out of hibernation!

**VELVET AND FEATHER
FANTASY INSPIRED BY A
17th-CENTURY
COURTIER'S CAP EVOKES
A BEAROQUE MOOD.**
Black feathers and gold-
trimmed black velvet, *inset
right*, combine to make this
chapeau by Coco Cubnel one
of the season's spellbinders.
It will leave him
bearethless!

**LET YOUR FEATHERS FLY
AS EVENING BRINGS OUT
ALL THE BEARS
OF PARADISE.**
Plumed and feathered, the
bear with panache in a
feathered and beaded mini-
dress, *right*, by New York
designer Bearry Ellis.
The only fragrance for
such extravagance is
Arctophile by Houbeargant.
Be a libeartine!

Does your love life feel like the stuffing's been knocked out of it? Is the thought of snaring another guy unbearable? The first step to trapping and keeping a he-bear is to identify what type of hugger you're after. Gals tend to think that their love problems are unique, but furry lotharios *do* fit into certain cubbyholes.

Teddy Types:
A Field Guide to Loveable Bears

By C.E. Crimmins

BESPECTACLED BEAR This preppy, studious cub is a tweedy type who can fall head over heels in love with any she-bear who reads *Bearron's* or knows how to sail. He'll often arrive bearing gifts of smoked salmon and the Sunday *Times*. He's a bruin who's much more secure about his brain than his brawn, but you can reassure him that girls *do* make passes at cubs who wear glasses!

CUB SCOUT That gung-ho guy who's always out for adventure. Boyish, irresistible—if he ever grew up, he'd probably be unbearable. This cubby is the most charming of the lot, but beware—he sometimes needs a den mother instead of a den mate.

PANDA BEAR A very straightforward fellow—everything's black and white with him. He'll never compliment you unless he really means it, and he'll never cheat on you because he values stability. Having more than one cuddle cub in his life would cause pandamonium.

POLAR BEAR His icy exterior scares off some cubbies, but he's been known to melt in the heat of a torrid romance. Polar's natural cool makes him an excellent businessbruin and terrific provider. If you're lucky enough to have landed this fine specimen of a bear, your igloo will always be fully equipped. (Romantic tip: Finding him slow to warm up lately? Feeling like you're polar opposites? Just rub your nose against his to rekindle the romance!)

BEARY GRANT That rare specimen of the male animal: A Black Tie Bear. He oozes class and is equally at home at the casino table or on the polo field. If you're secure enough to watch other cubbies' heads turn when he walks into a room, then you can handle a Beary Grant. Otherwise, watch out—she-bears will be on the prowl, and you might get your fur ruffled if your date rises to the bearbait.

GRIZZLY BEAR A curmudgeon whose growl is worse than his bite. This grizzled veteran of the love wars has mellowed into a grumbling bumpkin who needs a Goldilocks to come home to after a hard day of clawing his way to the top.

THE BEARCAT Reckless, daring—a hellion of a character with a hair-trigger temper, a scowl on his snout, and a growl in his throat. He picks fights, drives fast, and doesn't mess around with niceties. Wherever he goes, fur flies. Many a cubbie has tried to tame this rebel, but he'll never be muzzled. What to do if you're hopelessly in love with this type? Grin and bear it.

SLOTH BEAR This lunk's idea of fun is an afternoon watching Yogi cartoons or the Chicago Cubs. Still, if you can adjust to his low energy level, you'll find him kind, considerate, and affectionate in a fuzzy sort of way. Your challenge—to get him out of the den once in a while to work off his bearbelly.

BEAR-FACED LIAR A most dangerous beast, but often charming and sensual. He'll tell you anything you want to hear, even if it has no bearing on reality. This type of cub is great for a fantasy fling, but don't try to put a ring in his nose—he might have left another missus hibernating somewhere.

Teddy Types: A Field Guide to Loveable Bears

Reading Love's Bearometer: A Quiz

Are your notions about your romantic opposite pretty fuzzy? Or do you have knowledge to bring to bear on the subject of romantic love? Find out by taking our quick love test.

1. After discovering that my best friend's husband or lover is cheating on her, I
A. Keep quiet because I hate to be the bearer of bad news;
B. Call up the creep and threaten to maul him if he continues cheating on his honey;
C. Conquer my embearrassment and tell my friend, at the same time offering her my pad.

2. At a party, a friend comes up and tells me that a hunky cub definitely is eying me. I
A. Pooh-pooh the idea and go on talking to my brother-in-law;
B. Fluff my fur and casually walk in the direction of the guy and hope he'll notice me;
C. Make a beeline for Mr. Right and bear my soul to him.

3. It's my first date with a bearly respectable type, and he seems to want to spend it pawing me. I
A. Growl and get myself out of a hairy situation;
B. Tell him very calmly that I find him unbearable;
C. Put up with the bearrage of advances from the beast and then never see him again.

4. A mysterious stranger appears in my life who claims to be enamored of me. He reveals himself to be a Bearvarian bearon and he begs me to leave with him immediately and live in his castle. I
A. Hightail it down to the passport office;
B. Muzzle my feelings and begin a quiet investigation into his background;
C. Let him down gently by saying that the language bearrier would be too great for me to become a bearoness.

5. While stopped at a traffic light, I see a dashing-looking bruin behind the wheel of a vintage Beargatti. I
A. Come within a hair's breadth of honking my horn and waving my paw, and then forget all about him later;
B. Wait until the light turns and then aggressively bear left until he is forced to yield to me;
C. Take down his license number, lose it, and go bearserk thinking about him for weeks.

Answers: "A" answers are worth 5 points; "B" answers, 10 points; "C" answers, 20 points.
Scoring: 15–30 points—You are bearly interested in romance. Stay in hibernation!
35–70—You are one smart honey of a bear. As a cubbie you probably pelted your mother with questions about the bears and the bees, and learned how to avoid getting stung.
75–100—You're always sticking your snout where it shouldn't be, and as a result, you know the bear facts about romance. Have a growling good time!

Secret to a knockout body: Aerobearcize that strengthens and stretches, says Boris Bruin of Hollywood's trendy honey of a fitness salon—Body by Bruin

BEARABLE WORKOUTS!

● 1 Mini-Squats

Stand with feet forward, about shoulder width apart, paws on hips. Slowly bend knees, foot pads firmly on floor, then straighten up. Do 10 times, working up to 30.

● 2 Knocked-kneed Bends

Stand with feet further apart, knees held tightly together. Bend left knee forward, then shift your weight and bend the right. Do 10 times and slowly increase to 30.

● 3 Front Kicks

Stand with paws on hips. Or, for more support, place left paw against a wall or chair back. Slowly lift right leg in front of you (straight if possible!) with toe pointed upward. Do 10 repetitions. Then flex paw for another 10 reps. Repeat the entire sequence with the left leg. Work up to 40 repetitions per leg.

● 4 Back Kicks

Place left paw behind head. Place right paw on hip. Bend slightly forward and lift right leg up in back as far as possible. Keep the movement slow and controlled, raising leg only as high as you can without straining. Do 10 times with foot pointed; 10 times with foot flexed. Repeat with left. Work up to 40 repetitions per leg.

● 5 Leg Raises

Lie on the floor with paws behind your head. Keep back pressed tightly against the floor. Raise both legs straight up until they are perpendicular to the floor; slowly lower the legs until they touch the floor. Repeat five times and then sit up and touch your toes with your nose. Work up to 30 sets.

furry, firm and fabulous

37

"Don't hate me because I'm bearethtaking."

"This is my fur in the morning."

"So I have to wash it. And blow it dry. Just like every other cubbie coiffure. How come my fur looks beautiful despite all this? I discovered Pandatene. It helps me go from fury to furry.

You see, Pandatene scientists have developed a special formula. A provitamin, honey enriched, B-6 complex that actually penetrates fur to give it inner strength.

So it's strong enough to stand up to frequent washing. To blowdryers and brisk brushing. And even excessive hugging.

Look for Pandatene Honey Enriched Shampoo and Bodifying Conditioner at fine beartiques everywhere. Perfect for plush, marvelous for mohair."

"Your fur will seem silkier.
More Huggable.
    Unbearably Beautiful.
Just like mine."

PANDATENE
SERIOUS CARE FOR FABULOUS FUR

● Albeart Nipon wraps a white cotton piqué halter and matching zip-up pants in a shawl collar bubble jacket of khaki taffeta, *far left. Top near left,* pink, double-breasted jacket over a black mini and bustier. All by Bearry Ellis. *Center near left,* multi-colored wrap sarong by Bear Blass. Faux jewels by Van Cleef & Arbears. *Bottom near left,* roomy trousers with hand knit sweater by Teddy Lapides. *Bottom far left,* Irish knit sweater with hot pink chiffon scarf accent topped off with an oversized straw hat by Bearry McFadden. Star struck cubbies will select these bearry delightful ensembles for every occasion.

L.A. ACTION

HOT, HONEYDEWED AND UNBEARABLY BRIGHT

There's nothing laid-back about fancy dressing in the City of Angels. Here, a roundup of some of the brightest fashions that don't fit into any cubbyhole!

New fashion energy is ablast in the Golden State. A diverse group of creative cubbies—all in their 20s and 30s—are establishing their dens in L.A. rather than hibernating in cold-old New York. The result is style with a honey-honed West Coast edge.
California's cuddlesome cubs select honey-hued silks and chiffons that can be accessorized with hot, endless-summer colors.

SLEEK AND SOPHISTICATED...

URSA-MAJOR
Activated Honey with Trace Elements

No fur can afford to be without it.

To nourish your fur and help it to function more efficiently in today's stressful environment, Bearcôme labearatories introduces an extraordinary honey containing trace elements. The minerals essential to your fur's luxury. A few measured drops containing copper, iron, zinc, bearium, and magnesium progressively help restore your bearskin to its prime. Used daily, it increases the efficacy of your personal fur care regime. Your fur will show:

- a lustrous sheen for a more radiant, youthful look
- the vital effects of good hibernation
- a smoother texture and evenness of tone
- the sweet loveliness that comes from honey and 5 more of life's essential minerals.

Ursa-Major. Fortified formula for finer fur forever.

URSA-
MAJOR
Activated Honey with
Trace Elements

BEARCÔME
PARIS

BEARCÔME
PARIS

IN PARIS the trend is swept-back ears highlighted with oversized earrings. Some avante-garde teddies are accenting their eyes with streaks of shadow in muted tones. The rage is color as top designers like Yves Saint Bearent and Unbearo bear witness to their love of crimson hues. Red is everywhere and no right-minded cubby would be seen outside her den without a touch of flame in her fashion statement.

PARIS, MILAN
AND NEW YORK

INTERNATIONAL BEAUTY REPORT

The international scene is in a state of pandamonium as all the trendy bruins come out of hibernation for the new season.

IN MILAN hats are as bearoque as old castles and topping the list are gold lamé beehives that make even the shyest little honey bear a stinger!

IN NEW YORK the look of summer seems endless as Donna Bearran captures tawny sundrenched tones in every fold. But bear in mind: These looks are not intended for Ursa Minors—this is strictly major league!

A ROSE
BY ANY OTHER NAME

This season, everything's coming up roses. Suddenly, every designer's inspiration is that most exotic blossom of all — the legendary symbol of love and romance.

Now the fashionable teddy can express her heart's desire in shades of rose that range from dusty pink to crimson—the color palette includes the entire spectrum, from subtle to sizzling.

THE LITTLE BLACK DRESS REFRESHED WITH FLOWERS. THE BEARER OF PALE ROSES.
Strapless, fitted top, *left*, with a full, pouf skirt liberally covered with scattered roses. In silk by Bearlenciaga. The perfect fur moisturizer by Oil of Ours. The plushiest you ever!

A BOWER OF FLOWER SHAPES— A BEARETHTAKING BEAR BODICE.
A garland of silk blossoms, *right*, traces the neckline of an evening gown by Yves Saint Bearent. A crimson rose at the back of a black velvet pillbox—the combination is bearoque. Faux diamonds by Polara Picasso. The fragrance, Fleur des Ours by Fabeargé. Bee-stung nose powder by Cubnel. Bearably classic.

ONE OF THE MOST BEARLOVED FLOWERS, THE ROSE IS FLOURISHING THIS SEASON IN SOFT PASTEL SHADES. New drama in black velvet with a bare-backed gown, *left,* by designer Hubear de Givenchy. The deep plunging back is trimmed with oversized silk roses in soft pastel shades. Now you can go bearback. Ear clips by Bearry Winston. Eye shadow and nose poudre by Elizabear Arden. The shades are bearly visible.

44

FRESH FLOWERS AT ALL THE PARIS SHOWINGS MADE EVERY DAY MORE BEARABLE. Pure Parisian, *right,* the pale touch of pink used with black. Ursa de la Renta introduced a black chiffon bustier top with two flirty bows and a puffball skirt. The wide-brimmed jet black straw hat with a single silk cabbage-rose by Bearry Ellis. The effect, sheer pandamonium!

Grrrrr

rrrreat
eye looks now.

Color like never before; color to line your eyes and shade your brows.

What's bruin? New thinking: Unbearably beautiful colors in a dazzling array of shades that shimmer and highlite. Coordinated colors to line eyes and brush into your brows.

The look: Fun and frisky fashion. Right this minute. Maybearline's color experts proudly present a honey of a line in eight delicious combinations.

The concept: A color liner combined with a soft, silky brow brush. Now you can accent your eyes and brush highlighter into your fur right up to the brows.

New
Bear Image Brow Color and Eyeliner
Maybearline

Polara Picasso

FOR VENICE

VENICE sunglasses created by Polara Picasso.
One honey of an optical innovation.
Polarized, naturally.

the Blushing Bruin

**The new romantics —
ivory satin and chantilly lace —
caress and curve to create
poetry in motion**

bridal tradition decrees that there be something old, something new, something borrowed and something blue.

Satin and lace—
Ruffles and pearls—
Juliet-inspired charm—
The bearethtaking bride.
Traditional weddings are
back and that includes
the glorious gown. This
nuptial season inspired
Ursa de la Renta to
capture all the romance
of Juliet in a pearl
and mother-of-pearl
sequin encrusted gown.
The antique ivory
satin gown is trimmed
with heavy lace and
hand embroidered with
seed pearls. The Juliet
cap, *left,* is
trimmed in matching silk
blossoms and pearls.
This bearer of love
could melt any bruin's
heart.

Scattered blossoms—
Sweet Innocence—
This flower bearer
is a vision of loveliness.
Wide-eyed and innocent,
the flower bearer is
dressed in peach satin
trimmed with antique
lace. An Ophelia
garland of matching
blooms encircles her
head. Created by
Anne Ursine, this little
cubbie's first long gown
is a pure delight.

the
Blushing
Bruin

RICH CUBBIES

Free-spirited,
young cubbies
and romantic,
more mature
ursines
are padding
their paws
with the
fine
that
honey
can buy!

■ Gone are the days of paws that are simply shaved and coverings that are merely felt. Today's fashion-conscious teddy selects only the finest Ultrasuede and leather. Alternatives? Distressed leather, silk grosgrain and needle-pointed pads. A bearrage of nonconformist knockouts!

■ THE CRAFTY TEDDY PADS HER PAWS WITH ROMANTIC NEEDLEPOINT ROSEBUDS.

Bearly a wisp of a dress—rose-toned pink chiffon, *left*, by Hubear de Givenchy, is accented with rose-trimmed accessories. Straw hat and matching handbag by Bearry McFadden. A beareth of spring!

■ DELICATE TONED PLUSH EMBELLISHED WITH ELABORATELY EMBROIDERED FRENCH SILK GROSGRAIN RIBBON PAW PADS.

The ballgown trimmed in matching ribbon, *right*, by Albeart Nipon. Oversized ear ornaments by Coco Cubnel. The bearest hint of gold-toned eye shadow and plush blusher are by Elizabear Arden. Frankly faux fur by Bearglama. The ultimate expression of ursine opulence.

BEARLOVA

The Bruin.

The Legend.

The Fragrance.

BEARLOVA
PARIS
1988

Time-conscious teddy bears are beginning to realize that only they bear the blame if their personal lives go pelter-skelter. A new philosophy of togetherness is unfolding, and it starts in your own den. Don't cave in to outside pressures—create your own hideaway of love to escape the bearserk pace of modern living.

Create Your Own Den of Love

By C.E. Crimmins

It's called *cocooning*—a way to build a bearricade between you and stress while learning to enjoy each other's companionship again. With just a few modifications, your den can become a plush vacation spa where you'll enjoy hibernating on evenings and weekends. Afterwards, you'll return to the work world newly refreshed, ready to handle the barbearity of a competitive environment.

Decor should emphasize comfort, so get your couch cubby the best furnishings honey can buy:

- An upholstered wingchair worthy of any bearrister. The perfect seat for him to curl up in with pipe and slippers.
- A deep-pile plush rug—so luxurious that the two of you will want to relax bearfoot on it, enjoying the paws that refreshes.
- A Bruin espresso machine to make steaming cups of your favorite blend.
- A bear brick fireplace or old-fashioned woodburning stove where you can warm your haunches or cuddle for hearthwarming hours gazing into the glowing embears.
- A brass honey warmer to provide that perfect touch to Sunday brunch.
- Fold-away snack tables crafted of fine teakwood imported from Bearbados —perfect for informal fireside dining or those sweet moments you spend snacking on honey cakes and hot chocolate.

Need we go further? Whatever appeals to you soon ceases to be frivolous and becomes a bear necessity.

And what, as denizens of luxury, will you and your cuddle-cub do to pass the time? Sometimes nothing at all—it'll be a warm spot for woolgathering. But when the mood strikes, watch one of the many films recently released on home video for the bear market. Our favorites come from the Fur-Vid production company, which issues romantic old classics like *Cyrano de Beargerac* (starring Jose

Bearrer) and kitschy curiosities like Hanna-Barbeara film festivals and the many old episodes of the *Honeymooners* that bear repeat viewing.

And if you tire of the tube, why not revive the British custom of reading aloud to one another? Try a Dickens, like *Grrreat Expectations*—with such a place to come home to, you can't help but have terrific expectations for your own idle hours.

BEARING GIFTS:
Trinkets for Your Honey

All teddies need toys, and none can resist a female bearing gifts. Our suggestions for the he-bear in your life:

He'll know whether to get ready for outdoor activities or continue hibernating when he consults this handy

BEAROMETER. The perfect gift for the active sportscub, and its bearnished brass finish makes it a handsome addition to his den. ($79.95 at Bear Bryant Boutiques everywhere)

Every teddy should have the right to bear arms, especially this handsome **COAT OF ARMS** explaining the lineage of teddy bears everywhere. If his background has always seemed fuzzy, here's the clarification he needs! Hand-lettered on a rich background of dark walnut, it comes with a certificate of authenticity issued by the Greater Bearrington Genealogical Society. ($39.95 from Pawprinters, Inc.)

Get him into the swim of things with this high-tech **SCUBA BEAR-GEAR.** The mask, specially designed to fit snugly around the snout, will make him think he's snorkeling bear-faced. The view's terrific: Everything from angelfish to bearracuda. ($69.95 from The Sharp-Bear Image Catalog)

For the backyard honey who likes bearfoot cooking, how about a **GAS BEARBEQUE?** This one has one-paw ignition and such a large gas tank, it bearly ever needs refilling. He'll find it a sizzling accessory for outdoor entertaining. ($139.95 from L. L. Bear)

From Paris comes the essential chapeau for the ursinely inclined, the blue flannel **BEARET.** Cocked over one ear, it's guaranteed to give your amor a tres gallic bearing—what else could make a fella so furry handsome? ($29.95 from Bearre Cardin Designs)

THE GLOW OF GOLDEN HONEY

Midas touch: The rich feel of silky imported plush and gleaming mohair gives these coats of fur a discernible difference.

Feast your eyes on gleaming gold tones! You may have chosen it before as a shimmering highlight for that very special teddy. Now this golden delight can be an everyday affair. New technology makes the look and feel of luxury fur available at a mere fraction of its former cost. Golden tones are the quickest way to turn on style. Tawny shades for twilight make even the most sensible teddy heady. The perfect accessory: Gold-toned Ultrasuede paw pads with a monogram—spectacular!

SATIN-FINISH, GOLD-TONED MOHAIR— THE LOOK AND FEEL OF LUXURY.

A sumptuous white satin ballgown with oversize puff sleeves, *inset left,* by Bear Blass. White, bird-trimmed, satin Juliet cap with peek-a-boo veil by Calvin Ursine. Faux pearls by Van Cleef & Arbears. This white as snow, polar-inspired ensemble will make them paws and take notice.

HONEY-HUED PLUSH SHADED WITH BEIGE HIGHLIGHTS— PERFECT FOR AN ENCHANTED EVENING WITH THAT VERY SPECIAL BRUIN.

This high-waisted silk moire gown with flowing back panels, *right,* by Bearlenciaga is trimmed in black velvet and accented with oversized ear ornaments designed by Bearry Winston. The bear essence of romance.

57

THE ROMANTIC
LOOK OF SUNSETS—
PALE CHAMPAGNE
PLUSH HIGHLIGHTED
WITH DELICATE PINK
TWILIGHT TONES.
The evening gown, *left*,
with oversized bow, is
a sensation in shocking
pink. From the Paris
couture collection of
Yves Saint Bearent.
Faux diamond earrings
by Georgio Bearmani.
Be beardazzled!

BURNISHED ANTIQUE
GOLD MOHAIR
CAPTURES ALL THE
ROMANCE OF
OLDEN BEARS.
A sequined and feather-
trimmed fitted top over
chrome yellow and rose
red satin double-layer
skirt, *right*, by
Karl Lagbearfeld.
Oversized ear baubles
by Polara Picasso.
Shimmer Bruin shadow
and fur blusher by
Elizabear Arden.
Altogether a bearably
beautiful confection.

GEORGIO BEARMANI
NEW YORK • PARIS • BERLIN

DAYS OF WINE AND ROSES. THE LOOK OF FABULOUS FUR AT A HONEY OF A PRICE.
Plumrose is the newest shade of faux fur from Hubear de Givenchy, *right,* and these new tones suggest romantic fantasies that all little cubbies dream of. Being in this sensational cuddle coat will give you ideas that he-bears will pant to hear about.

FANTASY FURS

CUNNING COYOTE AND MAKE-BELIEVE MINK—
THESE PLAYING-POSSUM FOXY FAKES
ARE BEARLY BELIEVABLE.

There's nothing endangered about these look-of-luxury furs. Wraparound or full length, these cuddle-in coats are never overbearing.

LOOK OF LUXURY WHITE MINK WILL OUTFOX EVEN THE SLYEST LITTLE BRUIN.
Bank on this: Your nightlife will be filled with a bearrage of fancy invitations as you wrap yourself in this look-alike white mink stole, *right,* by Bear Blass. Trimmed with faux diamond clips and falling all the way to your feet, this luxury fake fur will gather the bruins as quickly as honey gathers bees!

NEW EVENING WRAP-UP: SWEEPING SILHOUETTES, LAVISH LONG-HAIR TEXTURES. GLAMOUR GALORE AS THE FAKE FURS ARE BARELY DISCERNIBLE FROM THE REAL THING!
Undeniably extravagant, the full-cut shape, *left,* with a grand oversized collar by Ursa de la Renta. The palest look of plush is achieved by shading with Bearly Visible powder shadow by Tedée Lauder. Get foxy with your big bad bruin in this make-believe mink.

63

Cover Cub presents a gallery of plush shadows to wear multi-colored, shade upon shade, blended or direct. From the sophisticated glimmer of art deco, to the romantic impressionist pastels. From the ultra-refined naturals of the Renaissance, to the brights of the modernists. Never overbearing. Panda the possibilities!

Cover Cub

There's a new
mood in Paris:
Softer, prettier,
more romantic.
And there's *color*!
Color galore!
This new palette is
often muted, but
when it's sharp,
it's offbeat and
sophisticated.
Brightly colored
bows and
glittering gems
add pizzazz.
Inspired by
sensuous lingerie,
glorifying the
body beneath,
black velvet and
black lace
curve and cling.
Bearly bare is
taking over!

naughty nights
paris
when it sizzles

SHIMMERY, SILKY, SEDUCTIVE—THESE ARE THE NEW
PARIS-INSPIRED LOOKS FOR EVENING. NIGHTS
PROMISE TO BE FULL OF NAUGHTINESS—THE FLASH
OF FUR UNDER FLIRTY DRESSES. THE IDEA IS TO SHOW
SOME PLUSH—BARE BEAR SHOULDERS, DÉCOLLETAGE
AND LOTS OF LONG LEG.

Bare assets revealed: The plunge. Décolletage that bares shoulders and bearly covers the bodice with bows. Bright red taffeta bows encircle the shoulders and add a festive note to evening wear, *left*, by <u>Bearlenciaga.</u> This dramatic effect is heightened by the tight-fitting bodice and opulent skirt.

Black chiffon and a
floral print create
romantic mood that is
e bear essence of a
erfect night.

immering flowers
vivid shades
t against a black
ckground, *left,* is
e couture creation
Yves Saint Bearent.
is off-the-shoulder
ess of delicate
k chiffon is trimmed
th embroidered floral
signs. The bearest
eeze makes this dress
em to float on air.
velvet leaf ear
nament in matching
ades completes this
areth of air
nfection.

Bewitching black
beauties: Two
r the night. Gowns
at glimmer with
t stones and
listen with faux
iamond accents.
ear in mind, this
ok is for bears
ho dare to bare all!
m satin gown, *far right,*
mmed with jet beads
er the bodice and
ound the shoulders
Cub Mackie for
earWear. Accented
th matching choker
d ear ornament, this
dy in black is not
r timid cubbies.
ack velvet gown with
versized satin ruffle
ccented with jet and
amond beads, *right,*
Hubear de Givenchy
a stunning example of
ntemporary bearoque.

paris
when it sizzles

Fur and fantasy! The lavish feel of luxury. The plush look of beadwork mixed with satin and fur-trimmed. Unbearably grand! The dramatic look of a plunging neckline suspended by beaded shoulder straps, *right*, by Christian Laclaw. The slinky satin gown clings and curves to reveal all that is bearable. The fur-trimmed, beaded stole, *far right*, wraps plush shoulders in luxury. The satin gown, with oversized bow in the back is by Bear Blass and is unbearably brilliant!

Black and bare Stunners either embellished with gold or touched with faux gems. An oversized bearette as accent! Noteworthy here is the sensuous shaping, *left*, created by the bias-cut skirt and accented with matching giant bow and gem encrusted beading trim. Paris original by Coco Cubnel. An armful of extravagant golden-yellow bows on black silk gloves, *far left*, accent a draped velvet floor-length gown by Bearre Cardin. The faux diamonds by Diane Von Furstenbear. A bearable feast of luxury looks.

paris
when it sizzles

The newest, hottest trend around? Fanciful chapeaus
in a vast array of colors and forms.
It's the season's best
bearightener.

TOPPING TEDDY

■ Flowered hats are blooming as the designer choice on all the runways this season. The most delightful are made of straw in rainbow shades. The most romantic: Swirls of pink tulle with clusters of bittersweet pink rosebuds. Humorous touches: A green parrot atop a red straw fedora covered with cascading bright berries. And a bit of stylish whimsy: A twisted turban beehive of shimmering gold-flecked tulle trimmed with tiny honeybees.

A GIANT ROSE ATOP A WIDE-BRIMMED STRAW MAKES THIS HAT AN URSA MAJOR.

A black, lace-covered wide-brim straw hat by Coco Cubnel, *left*, is accented by an oversized silk rose in shocking pink. The full veil adds a sense of mystery to this bearethtaking chapeau.

FLOWERS AND SPRAYS OF PEARLS MAKE THIS TOP HAT A WINNER.

Pink silk top hat decorated with a shaded wine-colored ribbon and matching blossoms, *top right*, by Anne Ursine is one of the season's best bearighteners.

HONEY BEES ARE BUZZING AROUND THIS TINY LITTLE BEEHIVE OF A HAT.

A beige silk beehive turban covered with gold metallic veiling, *bottom right,* by Bearlenciaga is the perfect bit of whimsey for any occasion.

GIANT POLKA DOTS AND OVERSIZED CHERRIES MAKE THIS BONNET PERFECT FOR A SUNNY SUMMER DAY.
This wide-brimmed silk hat printed in oversized navy polka dots and trimmed with huge red cherries, *top right,* is the creation of Bearry Ellis.

POLLY WANTS A CRACKER—THIS GREEN PARROT WANTS MORE THAN A FEW BERRIES TO MAKE HER DAY.
A red straw top hat trimmed with colorful berries and accented with a bright green parrot, *near right,* is the creation of Cub Mackie.

BLACK VELVET AND YELLOW ROSES MAKE THIS HAT PERFECT FOR ANY ENCHANTED EVENING.
Bright yellow silk roses trim this worn-to-the-side black velvet, narrow brimmed, top hat, *far right,* by Georgio Bearmani. A matching velvet bow adds to the festivities and sets this chapeau apart from the merely bearable.

A ROSE GARDEN OF BLOSSOMS ATOP A JET BLACK STRAW IS BOUND TO HAVE THE PANDAS PANTING. This garden of rose delights in multi-colored shades, *right,* by <u>Yves Saint Bearent</u> is sure to be a cubbie s delight.

Bearing a grudge against your mate? Is he toying with your affections? Our cub reporter on the romance beat provides answers to some hairy problems...

ASK URSULA

By C.E. Crimmins

Dear Ursula:

Once Ted could bearly get enough of me, but now I feel neglected. He's a stockbroker, and when he comes home, he gives me a quick nuzzle on the muzzle and then sits down to bury his snout in his *Bearron's* magazine until dinnertime. When I complain, he tells me that honey doesn't grow on trees.

Ursula, I know it's a bear market and he has to work hard, but how can I capture his attention once in a while?

Pining Away in Pawtucket

Dear Pawtucket:

I hear about your problem all the time. Face it—the working world's a bearpit. Some bruins just need time for wool-gathering when they get home so they can regain their bearings and start feeling amorous.

But in your case, spontaneity and romance have caved in to routine, and you'll have to take the bull by the horns (or the bear by the ears!) to get your love life back to a bearly acceptable level.

Stalk your love-cub just as you did years ago. Keep him off guard. Rent an elegant Stutz-Bearcat to whisk him away from the office to a romantic cabin in the woods, and bring along your bearest negligee—I promise you it will be one honey of a merger!

Q

Dear Ursula:

What do you think of this? In public, my guy can't keep his paws off of me. He's all longing looks and honeyed phrases when we're in a crowd. But as soon as we get home, the beast will have nothing to do with me. Why all the bruin ha-ha in public and so furry little at home?

Please don't use my name. Just sign me,

Wish My Love Den Were in Madison Bear Garden

Dear Wish:

I don't know what's wrong with your love-critter, but his behavior is barbearic! Public bearhugs and then nothing in private? Apawling! I'd say that this cub's notions of romance are fuzzy at best, and you shouldn't be expected to bear the brunt of his erratic bearhavior. Unleash the loser, and your love life will no longer seem like a three-ring circus.

Q

Dear Ursula:

My den mate isn't bearing up well to Father Time. In fact, you might say he's been snatched into the claws of a mid-life crisis. It all started with fur loss—he spent a fortune on that new drug that's supposed to grow mohair on his noggin. But even he realizes that they pulled the wool over his eyes on that one.

So now he's started on me. Ursula, he's becoming a kinky embearrass-ment. He's been taking Polaroid shots of me in my furry altogether on top of icebergs, and sometimes he dresses up as Smokey and "rescues" me from forest fires. Lately he's been trying to talk me into wearing a sequined muzzle when we cuddle.

Should I take him to a psychiatrist or just get him a set of bearbells to work off his excess energy?

Feeling Denigrated in Denver

Dear Denver:

You have nothing to worry about. At least you're not married to a Bluebear. He's living out his fantasies with *you*, not some furry young thing still wet behind the ears. Enjoy these last moments of passion as your cubby-hubby tries to push down the bearricades of middle age. Soon enough, he'll be padding around the house like Paw Kettle, and you'll miss the beast in him.

Q

Dear Ursula:

Every night, it's always the same thing. I serve Harry dinner and he yells, "Who's been eating my porridge?" He goes upstairs and bellows, "Who's been sleeping in my bed?" Then he begs me to get a blonde wig. What do you make of this?

Bewildered Bruinette

Dear Bewildered:

What can I say? Some bears lead a fairy tale existence.

CONFIDENTIAL TO PLEASINGLY PLUMP PANDA:

A guy who likes a skinny cubbie in a lacy teddy is never going to change. Don't be bamboozled. Ditch the diet koala and get on with your life.

BEARRY ELLIS

Share the best-kept secrets of the best-kept she-bears in Bearverly Hills.

JOSÉ EBEAR SALON

"**L.** is a cuddlecub who wants for nothing. Except, it seems, a case of imported honey to dip her petite paw into. I developed my Moisturizing Treatment Vital with HUNY to give dry, damaged plush new life, and to help protect it from rough hugging. She was so pleased with the results, she jumped into her vintage Stutz Bearcat and drove all the way to Palm Springs for another case of the bee's ambrosia."

"**C.** has a cave the size of Texas. And she likes to change her fur color as often as she changes her frocks. My Accenting Gel is specially formulated to give her any look she wants. From beige to honeyed bronze. From Cuddly to Ultra-sophisticated. From Cute Little Cubbie to Bruin-Something-Special. Bear with me baby, who would you like to be tomorrow?"

MOISTURIZING TREATMENT VITAL with HUNY

MOISTURIZING TREATMENT VITAL with HUNY

MOISTURIZING TREATMENT

"**I** want every she-bear everywhere to share my secrets to beautiful fur. Secrets that add lustre and shine. Secrets that revitalize dry and damaged fur. Secrets that will change you from unbearably dull to beareth-takingly beautiful."

Look for the José Ebear Fur Care Collection at better bearshops everywhere. It's the only famous name you need for famous fur.

Secrets from the Den of José Ebear.

Bare bears—
beauty now
TRENDS

EYES ONLY

The symbol of the season's changes in sunglasses—new mirrored "ursinemetrics" from Polar Optics by Bearre Cardin, *above*, that appear to the wearer like ordinary sunglasses, filters more ultraviolet light than any other lens. Seen everywhere in a variety of frames from classic aviator to new smaller-size "geometrics" —favored on all this season's runways, they're the plushest accessory around.

MEGA FITNESS

Get rid of those hibernation haunches and join the body fitness boom. LA's hot new workout spa is Body by Bruin. Exercise facilities on this scale mean everything from an outdoor jogging path to valet parking. Aerobearcize, stress reduction and yoga plus Nautilus equipment and—can you bear it—a polar swimming pool.

MAXIMUM EXPOSURE

The fashion focus is bareness. Translation at the couture collections—bared shoulders, décolleté, an expanse of exposed plush. Yves Saint Bearent, *top* and *center*, Calvin Ursine, *below*. How to deal with all this revealed fur? For nighttime looks brush in tinted powder. For more shimmer: Tedée Lauder's "Bearly Visible" face poudre with pearlized sheen...or a body powder; Polara Picasso's is gold-flecked.

BEAR ESSENCE

Once upon a time there were only the venerable perfume houses. Then came "signature" scents from the biggest names in fashion such as Coco Cubnel and Bearlenciaga. Today, what constitutes a stellar perfumer or "signature" is increasingly diverse.

Honey Grams, once just a household name for a nutritional breakfast, has announced the introduction of a honey fragrance. Spokesbruins for the company explain that the essence reflects the new attitude toward healthy living and smells like fresh outdoors. Woolit, long the selected cleansing liquid of all natural-fibre bears, has decided to market a fragrance spray that makes you smell cleaner than you are—thereby eliminating the drying effect of frequent sponge baths. "Scent is a powerful way to evoke style," remarks Bearnard B. Bruinish, marketing director of the new fragrance division of Golden Blossom. "We feel that the scent of honey and almonds evokes all that is primal in the ursine personality."

What becomes a Legend most?

Bearglama

Hedda Hopbear at the Movies

as reported to Steve Zorn

Trouble's bruin at the Tenth Annual Bear Mountain Filmarama Cinemathon, held each year at a different Bear Mountain den. This time, we find ourselves back in Colorado for the First Decade Retrospective. I wish I could say there's mohair than meets the eye, but industry insiders say it's just the usual tedium in teddydom. The high altitude is no doubt contributing to the fuzzyheadedness of the bruins in attendance, and it also might explain the embearassing entries.

Forget about thundering appaws—it's obvious that things aren't nearly so plush as they used to be in this industry suddenly gone bearish.

The surprise highlight of the festival is Bearyl Hannah, who was positively pelted with praise from all directions. Remember her in *Clan of the Teddy Bear?* Lucky for her, neither does anyone else—seems she's been slated to recreate the Polar Prentiss role in a new Bearamount Pictures version of *Where the Bears Are.* Don't be so quick to poohpooh the idea: Francis Furred Cubbola directs. Rumor sez Connie Furrancis' immortal theme song will be sung by none other than Bearbra Streisand. The question remains: Will Babs *ever* get her nose re-embroidered?

Not to be outdone by Cubbola, Steven Spielbear is planning *The Great Gatsbear,* the classic saga of the bearren lives of the ultra-plush written by F. Scott Fuzzgerald. (As Fuzzgerald's pal Grrnest Hemingway once wrote, "The rich are different from you and me...they have more honey.") Contenders for the male lead include *Bearfly*'s Mickey Roar (who may even have to shave off his three-day's growth of chin fuzz); *The Cotton Cub*'s Richard Bere (where's he been hibernating?); and Bearrison Ford (what *hasn't* he done?). The female lead? Spielbear isn't talking, but my sources say it's a close race between Broadway honey Bearnadette Peters and Grizzabella Rossellini, whose performance with the grizzly Dennis Hopbear (no relation to yours truly) in *Brown Velvet* wasn't mere fluff. Morgan Bearchild was up for this meaty part, but a claws in her contract with another studio forbids it.

Sequels? Have we got sequels! Already in the can are another *Rambear*; a new *Beverly Hills Cub*, starring Teddy Murphy; *Terms of Embearment—Part 2*; *Hannah and Her Cubs—A Second Look*; *Grizzly's Honor II*; another helping of *The Color of Honey*; and, in the current trend of dancers turned actors, still another remake of *Bear Geste*, this one starring Bearyshnikov (what a honey he is! When they made him, they lost the pattern).

My vote for the Leave-Well-Enough-Alone category goes to a new version of *Beary Poppins.* I'm not at libearty to divulge the casting choice for the title role, but suffice to say this rock star is known for wearing her teddy on stage and showing plenty of plush, and she's still licking her wounds from her latest theatrical embearassment, *Who's That Grr?*

The Hall of Fame selections were no surprise to anyone. Last year's film choice was *Cabearet.* This year the honor goes to *On Golden Blossom Pond*, starring Katharine Hepbearn and Henry and Jane Panda (who looks every bit as good as she does in her aerobearcize tapes—she still has the shape she showed off in *Bearbarella*!). Henry Panda was posthumously given the award for the biggest contribution to film art, following in the tracks of last year's winner, Ursine Welles, maker of the classics *Citizen Cub* and *The Magnificent Ambearsons.*

No film festival is complete without a little dirt, and when two beauties arrived wearing the same Saint Bearent, the fur fairly flew! Joan Koallins told Zsa Zsa Gabear to "get st_ffed," and both brawlin' bruinettes (if the truth be known) were unceremoniously escorted out of the convention hall. Meanwhile, on the other side of the *ours d'oeuvre* table, the clannish rock band *The Grateful Ted* felt compelled to prove they aren't stuffed shirts by ignoring the black tie requirement. Are these guys bruins or brutes?

That about wraps it up for the Tenth Annual Filmarama Cinemathon. Aren't you sorry *you* weren't there? Huggie-huggie, kissy-kissy till next!

Koalarizing the Classics

This year's Cinemathon heard a roar of protest from respected celebearties about that latest trend: Koalarizing the classics.

While some bruins embrace the idea with a big bear hug, opponents are virtually frothing at the mouth. Actor/politician Clint Beastwood, the torchbearer in the fight against koalarization, said, "The richness of black-and-white can't be enhanced by adding electronic color. The great early films of Greta Garbear, Joan Clawford, and Ingrid Beargman deserve respect." The star of the *Dirty Hairy* films took another swipe and growled, "The alteration of these and other films of our forebears is a cause for beareavement."

Actor/salad-dressing entrebruineur Paw Newman (who confided that he's about to market his béarnaise sauce) feels differently. "Koalarization," he explained, "makes old films more bearable for new viewers. Obscure films are saved from extinction. The works of famous actors like the Bearrymores and important directors like Sergei Eisensteiff will live on thanks to electronic color."

Is koalarization good or evil? Right now it's impossible to know; what we need is the opportunity to paws and reflect.

Bearre Cardin

bloomingbruin's

FLIRTATIONS

Witty notions augment high style: Feathered hats and bags, plus a bearly believable bounty of teddy togs that cannot be cubbyholed.

PURSES AND PLUMAGE

Feathers flew at the recent collections in Paris. Yves Saint Bearent's group of tropical bird chapeaus led a flock of fabulous fancies that drove the buyers bearserk! The trend-setter was a towering plumed hat perched precariously between the ears and set back on the head. Pillboxes were also featured by Calvin Ursine. Feathered evening bags and an Ultrasuede clutch in the shape of a honey pot created quite a stir at Cubnel. Bearlenciaga introduced chic teddy deco sweaters and pullovers with an elegant touch for evening. All in all, there's been a bearrage of ideas fluttering through all the collections.

● Feather flurry. *Top row from far left:* Tiny little feather pouch by Bearry Ellis; Saint Bearent's pink plumed hat and dress; Karl Lagbearfeld's feathered cap. *Left center:* Pillbox hat of ostrich and sheared coq by Bearry Ellis. *Left bottom:* Silver streaked black ostrich boa over black satin gown accented with an oversized diamond clip by Emanuel Unbearo. *Far left:* Two gold-toned tiny evening bags by Bearry Winston. Leather penny purse in the shape of a teddy bear by Calvin Ursine. A bearrage of feathery flights of fancy.

Quick change clutch:
Fashionable little teddy bag
holds just enough spare change.

CREATE A BEAR SENSATION

NEW FUZZAZZ SHEER COLOR WASH

INTRODUCING SEE-THROUGH SHINY
ALL-OVER COLOR

Why settle for being a brunette?
Change the color of your fur as often
as you fantasize with New Fuzzazz Sheer
Color Wash. 8 Sheer, dazzling choices to
put color power in your plush! All have
built-in conditioners. All wash out in
4 shampoos. It's bearly believable, it's
sheer madness not to go for more Fuzzazz!

WHO COULDN'T USE
MORE FUZZAZZ?

CUBIROL

● Fancy pants: Oversized palazzos with a brightly colored top, *far left*, by Bearry Ellis. Slinky black velvet bloused pant with flame red belted jacket, *near left*, by Bearlenciaga.

● Billow talk: This bearably light coat practically floats. In black silk organza with oversized pull-on pants in black taffeta by Bearry Ellis.

Now, pants are hotter than ever! The big news: Unlimited choices, from full-leg palazzos to honey-hot, sexy Capris in a bearrage of bold prints. Bear in mind that wearing pants has never been so much fun!

PANTING FEVER

LEGGY BRUINS BEAR OUT THE TROUSER TREND

This season ushers in a whole new era in pants, with staid solids giving way to innovative, vibrant prints. The Paris fashion bruins bear down hard on splash and splatter as dashes of color and abstract motifs create eye-popping delights. Energizing these bearry special looks (as if they need it!): Sporty little honey hats and lots of piled-on accessories. It's fashionable panting at its best!

HOROSCOPE

CAPRICORN
December 22 - January 20

The Capricorn bear will be sure to have a full stocking after all the Santa bears have been to visit. This is the season to make wonderful resolutions that are fun to break!

The January ladybear is steadfast, endlessly caring and an ambitious go-getter. Never mind that stolid surface and strong aversion to the limelight, this relentless cubbie climber spends years convincing her rivals that she's really no threat and then leaves them to bite her dust as she moves out ahead of the pack.

Curly locks are the crowning glory of the bear born under the sign of the goat—keep your pelt luxurious with frequent brushing. Hunky bruins will want to woo the Capricorn cubbie beside a waterfall or in the waiting room of Grand Central Station. Just leave the pandas panting—the January cubbie is no easy prey!

AQUARIUS
January 21 - February 19

The Aquarius bear will find the year ahead to be filled with wonder and delight as one magical moment after another fills her days and nights.

The February bear is a love cub who may have more stunning wit than analytical genius. But the water-bearer's charm and grace will take her anywhere she dreams of. No merely material cub, Uranus' cubbie isn't interested in cuddles for cuddle's sake, but a bruin with serious intentions and a good sense of humor could be her bear in shining armor.

This is the season to look and act casual with windblown fur styles and short skirts that will drive the boy cubs wild! Keep them panting with long black gowns that tempt and ignite. The Uranus ursine can play the vamp or the den mother—it all depends on what's bruin!

PISCES
February 20 - March 20

The Pisces bear will find romance early this season and her heart's desire will be sure-fire. This is the time to *be* serious and *get* serious—the party isn't over, it's just beginning!

The March bear is often mystically sensitive and possessed of a romantic ESP that drives the he-bears to distraction. Can she really read their minds? She seems to *know* all the places that need to be hugged.

Enchanted by the alluring power of fragrance—scented bath oils and dusty blossom scented powders, the teddy born under the sign of the Fish loves the sensation of fragrant moonlight bathing. Her taste in clothes is like her taste in he-bears—diverse. To woo and win her, the brainy bruin must suggest the improbable—a compartment on the Orient Express or a cabin by a lake. The delight is in the difference!

ARIES
March 21 - April 20

The Aries bear is due for some exciting changes that range from a new hair style to a new romance. This season promises to add sparkle to every occasion.

April's bear is a lovable cub with a curious mix of wide-eyed wonder and wondercub smarts that attracts the most unlikely set of bruins—everyone from the honey salesman to the culture cub. Big bruins beware: She'll snatch your honey and your heart—usually on a whim or a dare! High spirited Ram bears hurl themselves into love affairs, holding nothing back, but they are barely able to survive a broken heart or a broken promise.

Glitter and sparkle show off a Ram bear's ebullient good looks. Be unbearably beautiful in a slinky little cocktail dress with more than a hint of plush revealed. Frosted fur and rose-colored nose tip will leave the bruins bearethless!

TAURUS
April 21 - May 21

The Taurus bear will find herself surrounded with lovely things this season, including a dashing new bear beau and maybe—just maybe —a glittering band of gold for her left paw.

To the Venus-ruled cubbie, the feel of satin sheets, the beauty of fresh cut flowers, the smell of just-baked honey cakes, mean more than any abstract notion. Not that this bully bear can't match wits with the best of brainy bruins; on the contrary, her honest, down-to-earth approach often leaves the less firmly-planted types stuck in the mud. Love with this cubbie is more often like a roller coaster ride than a picnic in the park.

A winsome *gamine* look with short cropped fur and eyes enhanced with smoky shadow will keep the bruin beaus courting. Red satin and black lace are a winning combination for evening. Be bearguiling!

GEMINI
May 22 - June 21

The Gemini bear will find herself in a whirl of festivities this season as her appointment book is filled to over-flowing with exciting invitations.

The captivating June cubbie can charm any bruin out of hibernation with her quicksilver charisma. But the cubbie born under the sign of the Twins can be both coy and cunning. Illusion is a Gemini trick, so play it subtle with just a hint of your bear essence.

Primrose is a favorite shade for bears born under the rule of Mercury; choose a subtle shade for your nose tip or have your favorite seamstress whip you up a clingy satin *teddy* for evenings by the fireside with your special brawny bruin. Remember that right behind your fuzzy little ears is one of your best bearogenous zones.

CANCER
June 22 - July 23

The Cancer bear will find her home life a source of great pleasure this season as unexpected guests bring surprise and delight into her life. And one of these guests could be Mr. Right!

The July bear is a sensuous lady who would rather cuddle at home than party on the town. There's no place more inviting than the moon-maiden's kitchen, redolent with the aroma of honey cakes baking and herbal teas brewing.

Cubbies ruled by the moon have lustrous locks, so go easy on gels and mousse—good brisk brushing is all it takes to make your fur unbearably beautiful. A candlelight dinner at home can be as romantic as a corner table at your favorite bistro. Just remember to wear something bearwitching under your apron.

LEO
July 24 - August 23

The Leo bear will discover hidden treasures and secret talents this season as she explores the wonders of self knowledge. Indulge yourself in the wonders of you!

The August bear could light up Broadway with her megawatt smile, high-voltage personality, and electrifying charm. Ruled by the Sun, this cubbie has all the brightness and warmth of high noon. The ladybear born under the sign of the Lion is queen of all she surveys and rules with a toss of her mane.

This season the Leo cubbie can go *sauvage* with exotic imported silk prints acquired from out-of-the-way shops and accessorized with hand-carved beads from China and India. And when this teddy lioness cuddles her favorite man cub in a softly swaying hammock, she should remember to be gentle—very gentle!

VIRGO
August 24 - September 23

The Virgo bear will discover her romantic dreams are not just far-fetched flights of fancy as one hand-some bruin after another brings roses and honey to her door.

The September bear is intelligent, hardworking, and totally reliable, but she is also a dewy-eyed romantic capable of passionate raptures. Ruled by Mercury, this cubbie can change moods and styles with the speed of light. She can dazzle and delight just as quickly as she can demur and depart.

This season, long, dragon-lady paw-claws are *out*: Instead try shorter, rounded nails in pearlized translucent shades. Pretty, frankly female styles best display the Virgo bear's plushy charms. By day she's chic in a champagne wool suit—a froth of ivory lace at her bosom. In the evening add a veiled pillbox hat for a touch of mysterious allure. Wall Street bruins may feel bullish but to Virgo it's a bear market!

LIBRA
September 24 - October 23

The Libra bear is due for a change of pace this season as her love life heats up and her career takes a turn upwards. The days ahead are filled with excitement and one very special promise!

The October bear collects friends, lovers, and professional allies as easily as she breathes. Her sparkling wit, vivacious charm and honey of a disposition make her one of every season's favorites. Beware boys—when she cuddles up, you may be tempted to tell her *all* your secrets.

Now is the time for the daughter of Venus to upscale her image! Frizzy, permed fur is *passé*—invest in a good trim and styling. And for romance, take your special man cub deep into the woods for a carefree weekend hibernation in a cabin by a lake. And let nature take its course!

SCORPIO
October 24 - November 22

The Scorpio bear should be careful not to burn the candle at both ends this busy season. The time for romance is at hand and one very special bruin has a surprise up his sleeve!

The November she-bear is a dynamic enchantress whose keen intelligence and eerie insights make her a force to be reckoned with. Once ensnared by a Pluto-ruled seductress, heady bruins can never go home again! This Scorpio teddy unbears her shoulders but not her soul. Her favorite romantic rendezvous—the gym after closing or a dewy meadow at dawn.

This season the look is one of luxury as satin, diamonds, and floor-length mink dominate the fashion scene for Scorpio bears. Slip into something that will reveal your intentions and you'll heat up your manbear with more than a fire in the hearth.

SAGITTARIUS
November 23 - December 21

The Sagittarius bear will have a lot to be thankful for this holiday season as generous employers and bountiful beaus prove again and again that giving is better than receiving. Well, almost better!

The December bear can melt the frost off even the coldest heart with her sunny disposition and breezy candor. Big, strapping bruins drop in their tracks from her freewheeling approach to romance. She is no easy prey—the archer bear enjoys more than her share of exotic adventures.

The Jupiter-ruled cubbie is feeling free and frisky this season and is coming out of the woods with a startling new look. With caution tossed aside, she is tempting nature with a rosy new nose tip color and a frosted fur style. The back-to-nature look is *out*, this season's look is bold and bearethtaking. Don't sit at home and hibernate, get out and libearate!

WOOLIT FLAIR:

WHEN IT SHIMMERS AND SHINES, KEEP THE HONEY GLOW WITH WOOLIT.
The newest styles in the finest furs are shining everywhere. It's a brand new feel, and a brand new way to use Woolit. This fragrant formula refurbishes those furs without shrinking, stretching or fading. Woolit fragrant care goes with you whenever you migrate, from Boston to Berlin. Trust Woolit.

WOOLIT. YOU CAN TRUST IT.

● Warm and wonderful—the bold new patterns and yarns that make sweaters all the rage. Brightly colored patterns set against a black background, *far left*, make this over-sized wool sweater by Bearry Ellis a winner. Floral designs printed on corduroy, *left*, combined with cashmere sleeves make this cardigan by Coco Cubnel the perfect choice.

homespun appeal

Patterns for day, Pastels at night:
Unbearably beautiful knit hits!

WILD AND WOOLY SWEATERS

Nowadays, a bear's best friend may be a lamb as fashion decrees that sweaters are big news —the bigger the better. Oversized both in size and pattern, the newest look in pullovers and cardigans is wild color by day and tame pastels for the evening. Baa, baa, brown bear, wrap yourself in wool!

CUDDLE UP WITH THIS SEASON'S WOOLY WINNERS

● Pure wool embroidered with pearl beading, *above*, by Emanuel Unbearo is the stylish choice to wear with a plaid wool skirt and scarf. Bright blue hand-knit sweater, *below left*, designed by Bearry McFadden is a classic style for every occasion.

Mousse FurFluff

Possibly the most bearable fur style you'll ever wear.

Touch it. So Perfect Mousse FurFluff feels like the most luxurious cloud of imported plush. Gives you an incredible sensation as your paw glides over the satiny surface of your precious pelt. It lets your fur breathe. Result? A perfect, fine-textured finish that looks fresh for hours.
And hours.

And very little goes a long way. So Perfect Mousse FurFluff applies in a measured amount so there's no guesswork, no waste—just So Perfect FurFluff. Natural. Glowing.

Elizabear Arden

PLUSHOLOGIST, HIBERNATION TESTED

WHO'S WHO IN BEARZAAR

▲ By Cindy Martin

In 1903, when Teddy Roosevelt refused to shoot a tiny bear cub, a legend the size of Paul Bunyan was born. Americans love folk heroes, and our history is peopled with romantic figures like Paul Bunyan and his blue ox as well as charming naturalists such as Johnny Appleseed. Often we don't know which characters are real and which are fictional.

In fact we *do* know that there was a hunting trip involving Teddy Roosevelt and a bear, but just how big and how young or old that bear was is still clouded in the romance of folklore.

In much the same way, the first teddy bear's origin is also obscured by the romance of folklore. Certainly the cartoon drawn by Clifford Berryman about the hunting trip, and all his subsequent cartoons that featured Roosevelt and the little bear helped to create the fever for stuffed toy bears named "teddy."

Two companies claim to be the first to market toy bears. In Germany, in 1903, the Steiff Company was making bears as well as other stuffed animals. In America, the Ideal Toy Company, inspired by the Berryman cartoon, began making bears as well. Looking back it seems unimportant to know who was first in the race, as the winner clearly seems to be the bear itself.

Of all the childhood toys, the teddy bear and the doll are the most celebrated. In terms of books and stories, the teddy bear has inspired many writers to create such classic fictional bears as Winnie the Pooh and Paddington. It is interesting that the

▲ By Marcia Sibol

bear, so ferocious in reality, is so benevolent in fiction. The bear stands alone as the only animal in folklore that is never a villain; while Walt Disney has occasionally created a bumbling bear, he has never created a vicious one.

Today millions of teddy bears share the lives of their human companions all around the world. There are national organizations that have selected the teddy bear as their symbol, and recently teddy bears have joined the police as helpers for distressed and abused children.

▲ By Mary Holstad

In 1983, when I wrote *The Teddy Bear Lovers Catalog,* there were only a handful of books available about teddy bears. Today, bookshelves are crammed with all sorts of books about teddy bears and the love that people feel for them. In 1983, there were just a half dozen or so teddy bear conventions. Today, hardly a week goes by without a teddy bear convention or show and sale somewhere in the world. Back in 1983, there were about fifty recognized teddy bear artists selling handmade bears. Today there are hundreds of teddy bear artists, and three years ago a professional artist guild was formed to gather and exchange information.

In August 1987, the American Teddy Bear Artist became recognized as a viable, creative force in the world of handmade art. The prestigious New York City craft gallery, *Incorporated,* opened its doors for the first exhibition of teddy bear art. By every standard the show was a success and the little children's stuffed toy became recognized as an art object.

The artists represented in this book are but a handful of those working today across America. Frankly, I selected these artists to make special bears because they are my friends and because I respect their work. Several of them are so successful that the waiting time for one of their bears might be over a year. And their work, when it is available, often sells for hundreds, even thousands, of dollars.

But all of them accepted my challenge to create a special fashion bear: a bear like none they had made before. The results far exceeded my wildest expectations. Without their creative energy, this book never could have been done.

All the artists represented here are presently making bears for shows and shops. They are all *working artists* who strive daily to create original designs. In this, they are no different from painters or sculptors, weavers or potters.

Many of the artists work long, tedious hours filling orders, and many support themselves and their children entirely by making bears. Not many artists, in any field, are able to do that.

Personally, I enjoy making bears and I love being around people who make bears, too. There is a special fellowship that cannot easily be described. It is, perhaps, a fellowship of love and mutual pain—we all suffer backache and sore fingers. And there seems to be more joy than envy when one of us does well—is singled out or wins a prize. That is very, *very* special.

In that spirit I wish to single out two artists. Beverly Port is one of the most versatile artists in the field. Often called the mother of the teddy bear artist movement, Beverly was the first to lift teddy bear making to the level of art. She is an inspiration to all of us. In the midst of a demanding schedule she not only made special bears for this book but several beautiful costumes as well. It is with great appreciation and affection that I thank Beverly for her contribution.

My friend and mentor, Diane Gard, is one of the more successful, self-supporting, teddy bear artists. Not only is Diane an accomplished artist, she is a consummate professional. She finds time to publish a newsletter which every one of her customers receives, and she writes articles for several of the teddy bear publications. If I could be even half as organized as she is, my life would seem utopian. When you ask an organized person to interrupt her schedule to make you a special bear, you are, I think, taking your life in your hands. But Diane worked extra hours to produce not just one but several fashion bears. She also became my main supporter during this project, and she kept me updated on the shows and other events that I had to miss in order to keep my own tight schedule. Thanks, Diane.

▲ By Beverly Port

There are always people behind the scenes who make a project easier. All of the staff at Running Press made every day more bearable, but to Nancy Steele and Steve Zorn, who acted as my editors, I owe a special debt of gratitude.

Thanks to C.E. Crimmins for her wit and insight that were smoothly applied to the world of teddy bears as sweetly as honey is spread on bread.

And thanks to June Amos Grammer, who interrupted her busy schedule to create the delightful illustration for Teddy in a Teddy. After working many years as a commercial fashion illustrator, June turned to the world of dolls and teddy bears where she now designs and illustrates products and books about her cuddlesome friends.

To Kevin Hastings, a thank you for the hours spent searching with me for props and accessories in every flea market we could find.

And finally, thanks to two very special ladies in my life who have cheered me on year after year, and who lent me their best hats, furs, and jewelry for this project. The fashion bears and I thank you both, Joan Shiel and Jeannie Sakol.

The following artists created fashion bears especially for *Teddy's Bearzaar:* **Doris Beck, Jane Carlson, Corla Cubillas, Suzanne DePee, Tatum Egelin, Barbara Ferrier, Diane Gard, Mary Holstad, Suzanne Marks, Cindy Martin, Beverly Port, Marcia Sibol, Barbara Whisnant.**

The following artists are represented by bears from the author's collection: **Deanne Brittsan, Georgia Carlson, Flore Emory, Judy Hill, Lynette Irwin, Judy Kruse, Kathy Mullin, Muriel Townsend, Suzanna Tyler, Lorna Wells.**

All of the bears shown in *Teddy's Bearzaar* are original designs and are protected by copyright in the artist's name.

All of the fashions were created by Ted Menten unless otherwise noted. Original fashions copyrighted in the artist's name.

▲ By Diane Gard

ABOUT THE AUTHOR

Ted Menten was born in 1932 on June the 12th, which makes him a Gemini. According to astrologers, that means he has a multifaceted and creatively diverse personality. It is, at best, the sign of versatility, variety, and a little bit of magic. P.T. Barnum was a Gemini.

Growing up as an only child among a host of artistic friends, family, and neighbors, Ted quickly developed an interest in art and began drawing and painting at a very young age. His first ambition was to be a fashion designer, but his father did not approve because, in his words, it was a "cutthroat business." Ted's second dream was to work as a cartoonist or animator. In 1951, he went to Hollywood to work for Walt Disney. At the end of a year he became homesick and returned to New York City.

After a few months of freelance design work, he was hired by Helena Rubinstein, the reigning queen of cosmetics, as a package designer. For the next twenty years, Ted designed packages for most of the leading cosmetic companies. By 1970, his design firm employed over fifty designers.

During this period, Ted began creating toys for some of the major American and European companies. Toys soon became his number one interest, and by the end of the 1970s he had amassed an enormous collection of dolls and bears.

During this period, Ted also created art and craft books for Dover Publications and wrote articles about collectibles for *Dolls* magazine. Then, in 1983, his life changed completely.

After years of living with teddy bears (which, as he explains, "everyone gives you if your name is Ted"), he decided to publish a book about his fuzzy companions. The result was *The TeddyBear Lovers Catalog,* first published in 1983 and currently issued in American, British, and Japanese editions. His photographs of teddy bears also have been published in the *Teddy Bear Lover's Postcard Book*™.

In another book, *The World According to HUG,* Ted features his cartoon character, HUG, a teddy bear of great charm and wisdom. Today HUG, HUG JR., BABY HUG, and Hug's Bear BUDDY are all available as plush toys manufactured by the North American Bear Company.

In all, Ted has written 12 books on his plush pals, and he currently is the editorial and creative force behind *Teddy Bear Review,* the quarterly magazine published by Collector Communications.

After years of designing, collecting, and writing about teddy bears, Ted decided in 1987 to enter the world of teddy bear artists by creating his first totally handmade bear.

"I knew that it wouldn't be easy, and I'd heard all the stories about backache and sore fingers and the endless frustra-

tion of getting things *right,*" says Ted. "But even with all that, it was the best thing I ever tackled, and I know that if my hands and my back hold out, I'll be making teddy bears for the rest of my life."

Ted feels that in many ways, *Teddy's Bearzaar* is the culmination of all his experience in designing cosmetic packages and doing what he calls "beauty head" photography—artistry that he has applied to his love of hand-made teddy bears to create the world of fashion bears.

"I always believed all those people who said that dreams do come true and that if you wanted anything enough you could have it if you worked hard and were patient. Well, they're right. After all these years I finally got to be a fashion designer and—what wonderful, patient, and delightful models these lady bears are. If you accidently stick one with a pin they never say a word—they just grin and bear it!"

ABOUT THE WRITERS

C.E. CRIMMINS is the author of *The Secret World of Men; Entre Chic: The Mega-Guide to Entrepreneurial Excellence;* and *Y.A.P.: The Official Young Aspiring Professional's Fast-Track Handbook.* She lives in Philadelphia with her husband, three cats, and a Pooh Bear.

STEVE ZORN is an editor and freelance writer who is allergic to mohair. He lives the plush life in Philadelphia.